Mario Chalmers'

ABCs
of
BASKETBALL

DREAM BIG. THINK BIG. PLAY BIG.

Mario Chalmers and Almarie Chalmers
Illustrated by Emmanuel Everett

www.ascendbooks.com

Mario Chalmers'
ABCs
of
BASKETBALL
DREAM BIG. THINK BIG. PLAY BIG.

DEDICATIONS

A special thank you to Dorena Montgomery, my 11th-grade teacher
at Bartlett High School in Anchorage, Alaska,
who gave a simple class assignment and, upon completion,
encouraged me to do more with it. Well, this is it!
To all of my family, teammates and coaches,
who helped me through the years.
But most of all, to the great game of basketball -
for being such an important part of my life.

— Mario

A special thank you to all of our family and friends
who assisted us on the road to completing this project.
It's yet another example of not giving up on your dreams,
as they do come true.

— Almarie

Hi, it's great to meet you.
My name is Mario,
but my friends call me Rio.
I hope you will, too.

So tell me,
what do you like to do?
I like hanging with my buddies,
and we always have a lot of fun.

Our favorite thing to do
when we get together
is playing basketball.
We do this more than
anything else.

Every single day, I practice hard.
Over and over, I dribble and shoot.
I'm developing fast hands and faster feet.
Ballin' is always on my mind, even when I sleep.

"Dream big, think big, play big!" That's what my coach always says.
He tells us it's how we should live our lives, on and off the court.
Coach always let's us know this is how we will achieve our goals

I'm going to tell you my dream: One day, I'm going pro – all the way to the NBA! I know that it's going to take a lot of hard work, and a lot of dedication. But I believe in myself, and I know that I'll get there.

I'm really glad you stopped by because I'm starting a new game. Are you in? It's called "The ABCs of Basketball," and it's the basics of the game from A to Z. Are you ready? Here we go!

Stick with me, and you'll be the newest member of my team!

A is for... ATTITUDE!

You'll need a positive one
when you play.
You should always feel great
about yourself, your teammates,
and your game.
Success begins
with the right Attitude!

B is for... BASKETBALL!

It's called a lot of different things, like rock, b-ball, or pumpkin.
Without it there's no game. When the Basketball goes through the hoop,
points go on the scoreboard!

Whether in a gym, on a driveway, or at a playground,
it's where we play the game.
It can be made of hardwood or cement,
and found indoors or on the street.
The Court is home to the game!

D is for... DUNK!

Jam the ball through the hoop,
and the crowd goes wild.
It can be one-handed
or from an alley-oop.
Jump high,
soar to the basket,
and Dunk like a superstar!

E is for... EFFORT!

It's giving all you've got.
Even when you're tired, keep trying,
keep hustling, and keep playing to the max.
Effort is doing your best, and giving it your all!

F is for... FREE THROWS!

These are the shots you get when you're fouled.
Go to the line, keep calm, and take a deep breath.
Set up your shot, and remember how you did it in practice.
Watch as you sink your Free Throws!

**They're what we all want to achieve. Dream big, and you'll play big.
Set your Goals to work hard, believe in yourself,
and don't let anything stand in your way!**

H is for...
HOOK SHOT!

It's great to watch,
and tough to make.
With practice,
this might become
your favorite way to score.
Arch your arm,
set your feet,
and let that
Hook Shot fly!

I is for... INBOUNDS!

This is where the ball is needed to start the play. The referee is counting, and time is running out. You must find your open teammate. Pass fast, get the ball Inbounds, and watch him make the shot!

J is for...
JUMP BALL!

It starts off every game.
Two players face off
as the referee
tosses the ball.

Reach as high as you can
for the Jump Ball,
and tap it
to your teammate!

L is for... LAYUP!

The most basic shot to learn,
but not always the easiest to make.
Take it to the hole,
because scoring is the
name of the game.
With practice and concentration,
a Layup will always
be there for you!

M is for... MAN-TO-MAN!

It's a way to prevent the other team from scoring. Your job is to guard just one player, but it's not an easy task. Playing Man-to-Man means that you'll need to be aggressive and focused!

N is for... NUMBER!

You wear it on your jersey, and it makes you one of a kind.
It's like having another name and is a source of pride.
My favorite Number is 15, and it motivates me to play my best!

O is for... OFFENSE!

The part of the game when your team has the ball. Play smart, listen to your coach, and work with your teammates.

On **Offense**, you can create and score points, and even hit the winning shot!

This is what makes perfect.
When the game starts, you must be ready,
or you won't be able to do your best.
Practice is the time for getting yourself
and your teammates set to compete!

2:14

HOME **1** 2 3 4 GUEST

— FOUL —

33 1 3 28

Q is for...

QUARTER!

This is a way to divide the game,
just like they do in the NBA.
You can think of a game
as four smaller ones,
and try to do your best in each one.
A Quarter is a reminder that
every second truly counts!

R is for... REBOUND!

When a shot is missed,
any player can grab the ball.
Box out, jump high,
stay focused and be brave.
A Rebound can be just as
important to the success of your
team as any points scored!

S is for... STEAL!

If you do it in basketball, that's a good thing and perfectly legal.

Watch for an opening, and then quickly move in to take the ball.

A **Steal** turns defense into offense, and gives your team a chance to score!

T is for... THREE-POINTER!

This is a shot that can make or break a game. No other basket is worth more, or more difficult to hit because you're a long way from the hoop. Get behind the arc, and let your Three-Pointer soar!

V is for... VICTORY!

This is your goal, and it's what you and your team are always trying to achieve.

Dedication, perseverance, and patience will be needed. With Victory comes the feeling that hard work has truly paid off!

W is for... WILLPOWER!

The self-control
that keeps you pushing,
striving to be the
best that you can be.
You must have this
to be a great player.
It's what makes you
practice and play harder.
Willpower is the
fuel of greatness!

X is for... X's AND O's!

Your coach will draw up plays for your team using these letters.
You'll see where you need to go, and where you need to stay.
X's and O's will show you who is who on the court.

Y is for... YOUTH!

It's the time in life when we're kids,
and when we're always ready to learn and play.
Success in basketball and success in life
is built during these years.
Enjoy your Youth, and be sure to have fun!

Z is for...

ZONE DEFENSE!

It's a type of defense where you guard an area rather than a player. Cover a specific space on the court, and anyone who enters it. Zone Defense requires confidence in your teammates and yourself!

It was really great to meet you, and I'm happy that we're now friends. But more importantly, we're on the same team.

I hope you had fun learning about my ABCs of Basketball. I definitely did!

Basketball is the best, and I just can't get enough of it. The game is such a huge part of my life!

My faith and my goals also drive me to fulfill my dreams.

I know that I'm still young, but I dream big, think big, and play big. And because of this, I'm unstoppable!

And you can be, too.

Until then, I'll just keep on sweating, playing and striving.
I won't give up— ever. And neither should you!

I've been living the "ABCs of Basketball" since I was in high school. Once I had written them down, I never forgot them.

In my basketball career, I've won two high school state championships, an NCAA National Championship with the University of Kansas and two NBA Championships with the Miami Heat.

The ABCs became my foundation for success as I moved through high school, then college at the University of Kansas, and then to the NBA.

I've always believed in myself, and relied on faith, hard work and dedication. Those qualities have made me who I am—as a basketball player, and as a person.

As you journey along with me through the pages of this book, my effort is to truly inspire you to become the best that you can be... on the court and off.

Deep down, I'm still young "Rio"—the kid with a huge dream who knew that with the right attitude and work ethic every goal could be achieved.

ABOUT THE AUTHORS

Mario "Rio" Chalmers acquired his love for basketball at age 2 thanks to a Nerf basketball and hoop, and brought home his first championship trophy from the local YMCA league at age 12. In high school, under the guidance of his father and head coach Ronnie, Rio won two Alaska State Championships, and was named as a McDonalds All-American. At the University of Kansas, Rio earned a starting position during his freshman year, and helped lead the Jayhawks to the Big 12 Conference title. Two seasons later, Rio was a key member of KU's National Championship team, and famously hit a 3-point shot with 2.1 seconds left in regulation of the title game, which has come to be known as "The Miracle Shot." Rio's success has continued throughout his NBA career, winning back-to-back championships with the Miami Heat, and as a standout with the Memphis Grizzlies. Off the court, Rio is the founder of the Mario V. Chalmers Foundation, which supports the positive development of youth through sports and education, and also funds breast cancer research and treatment initiatives.

Almarie Chalmers is a certified professional life coach, as well as Mario Chalmers' proud mom. She's the founder of Speak Life (life-coaching for women), and the annual Speak Life With Word luncheons, which offer exhortation to women, focusing on mothers and female cancer survivors. Almarie married her childhood sweetheart, Ronnie, and together, raised their son, Mario, and a daughter, Roneka, a graduate of the University of North Carolina-Charlotte. Additionally, Almarie serves as executive director of the Mario V. Chalmers Foundation, and helped develop Mario's Closet, at Lawrence Memorial Hospital in Lawrence, Kansas. A 20-year veteran of the Anchorage (Alaska) School District, Almarie still finds time to work on her writing and attend her son's games. Her first book is titled, "The Ball is in Your Court."

mario
MARIO V. CHALMERS FOUNDATION   www.mariovchalmersfoundation.org

ILLUSTRATOR

Emmanuel Everett has always been an avid daydreaming doodler. Since early childhood, Emmanuel has known that the stage was set for a lifetime of creative cultivation. Growing up in Anchorage, Alaska, provided a unique landscape and culture that further inspired his artistic approach to life. Whether creating and designing alongside small businesses or Fortune-500 companies, he continues to establish a progressive presence as a young artist and designer. Emmanuel strives for continuous growth and exploration... creating one big idea at a time.